THE TIME WIPE-OFF BOOK

SCHOLASTIC INC.
New York Toronto London Auckland Sydney

HOW TO USE THIS BOOK

1. Look at the SAMPLE CLOCKS on the next few pages; they show the positions of the hands, and how many minutes they are equal to, either before or after the hour. (HINT: The small hand always points to what hour it is.)
2. After you have studied the clocks, fold the flap on the back over the answers. Start with the HOUR page first, and begin telling time.
3. Write your answers in the boxes **with a grease pencil or an erasable felt-tip pen.**
4. Check your answers. How did you do?
5. If your answers are correct, erase them with a damp cloth and go on to the HALF HOUR page, and so on.
6. If you missed some answers, go back and review the SAMPLE CLOCKS, then try the same page again.

GOOD LUCK!

ISBN 0-590-45693-8

25 24 23 22 21 20 19 18 17 16   6 7/9

Printed in the U.S.A.
First Scholastic printing, August 1992

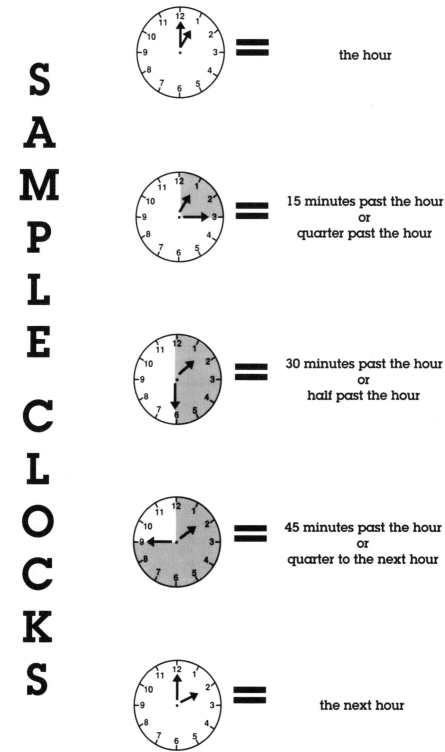

S A M P L E C L O C K S

the hour

15 minutes past the hour
or
quarter past the hour

30 minutes past the hour
or
half past the hour

45 minutes past the hour
or
quarter to the next hour

the next hour

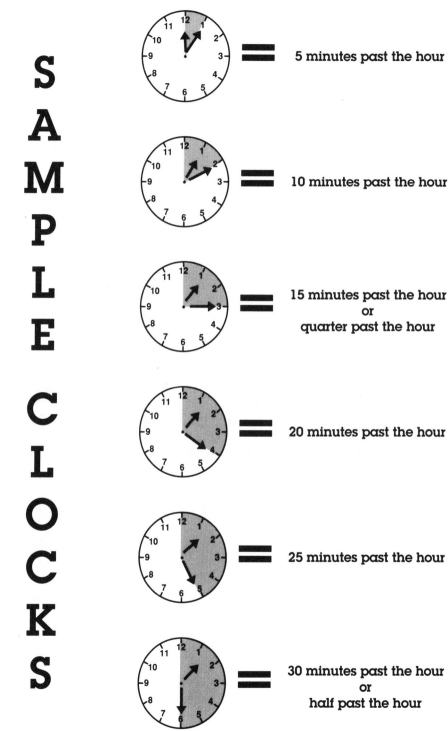

S
A
M
P
L
E

C
L
O
C
K
S

5 minutes past the hour

10 minutes past the hour

15 minutes past the hour
or
quarter past the hour

20 minutes past the hour

25 minutes past the hour

30 minutes past the hour
or
half past the hour

**S
A
M
P
L
E**

**C
L
O
C
K
S**

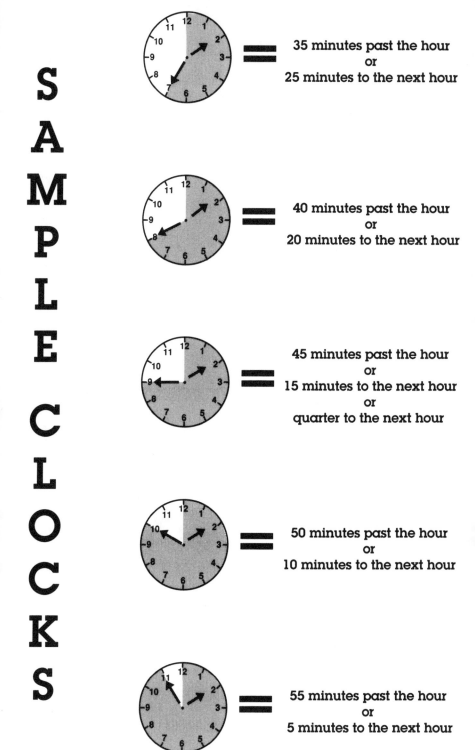

35 minutes past the hour
or
25 minutes to the next hour

40 minutes past the hour
or
20 minutes to the next hour

45 minutes past the hour
or
15 minutes to the next hour
or
quarter to the next hour

50 minutes past the hour
or
10 minutes to the next hour

55 minutes past the hour
or
5 minutes to the next hour

What Time Is It?

= 3 o'clock
3:00

= 6 o'clock
6:00

= 9 o'clock
9:00

H

O

U

R

= 4 o'clock
4:00

= 7 o'clock
7:00

= 2 o'clock
2:00

= 11 o'clock
11:00

What Time Is It?

= half past 1
1:30

H

= half past 10
10:30

A

= half past 4
4:30

L

= half past 5
5:30

F

= half past 2
2:30

H

= half past 8
8:30

O

= half past 3
3:30

U

R

What Time Is It?

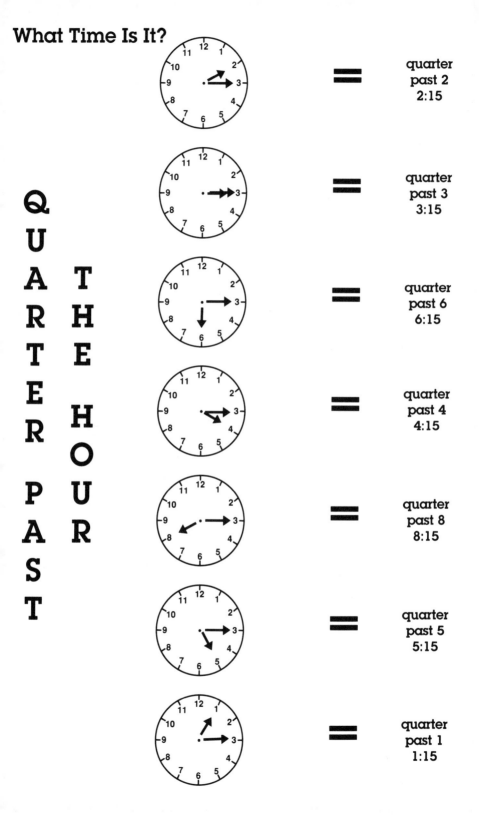

quarter
past 2
2:15

quarter
past 3
3:15

quarter
past 6
6:15

quarter
past 4
4:15

quarter
past 8
8:15

quarter
past 5
5:15

quarter
past 1
1:15

What Time Is It?

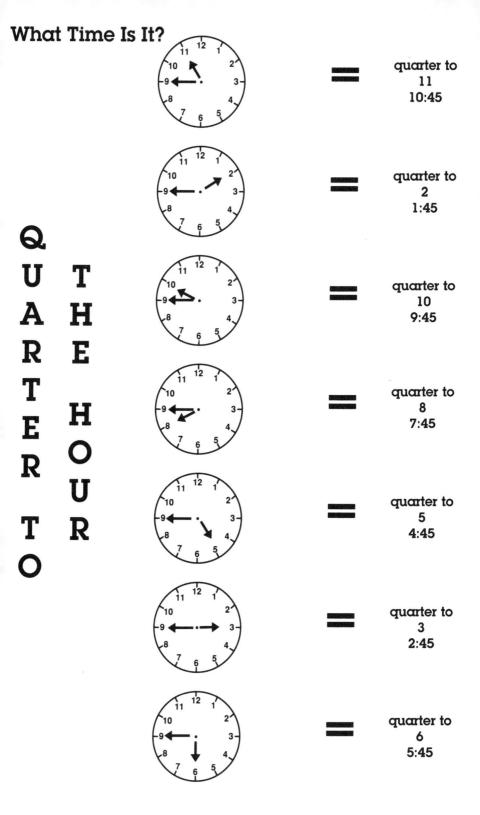

QUARTER TO

THE HOUR

= quarter to 11 10:45

= quarter to 2 1:45

= quarter to 10 9:45

= quarter to 8 7:45

= quarter to 5 4:45

= quarter to 3 2:45

= quarter to 6 5:45

What Time Is It?

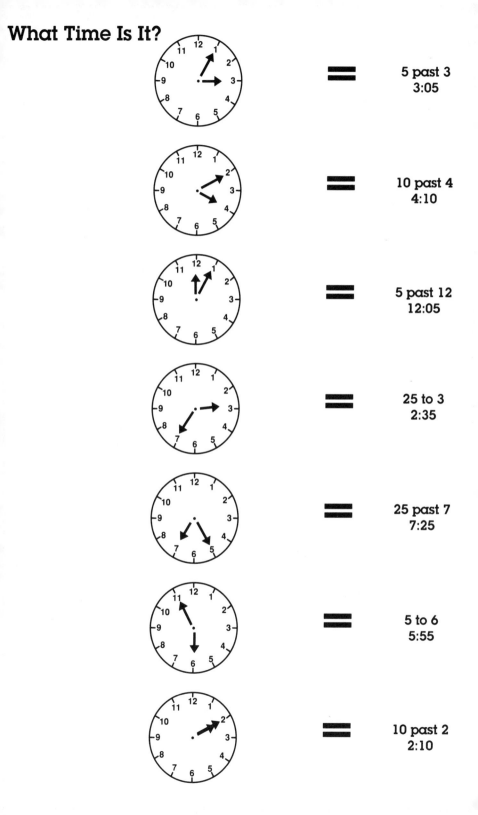

≡ 5 past 3
3:05

≡ 10 past 4
4:10

≡ 5 past 12
12:05

≡ 25 to 3
2:35

≡ 25 past 7
7:25

≡ 5 to 6
5:55

≡ 10 past 2
2:10

What Time Is It?

= quarter to 4
3:45

= quarter past 7
7:15

= 25 past 12
12:25

= 20 to 2
1:40

= 25 past 11
11:25

= 10 to 3
2:50

= 5 to 9
8:55

What Time Is It?

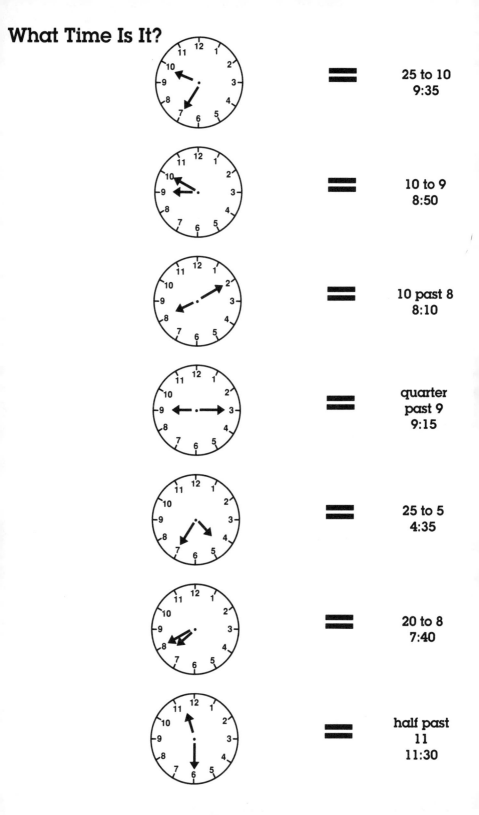

=   25 to 10
     9:35

=   10 to 9
     8:50

=   10 past 8
     8:10

=   quarter
     past 9
     9:15

=   25 to 5
     4:35

=   20 to 8
     7:40

=   half past
     11
     11:30

What Time Is It?

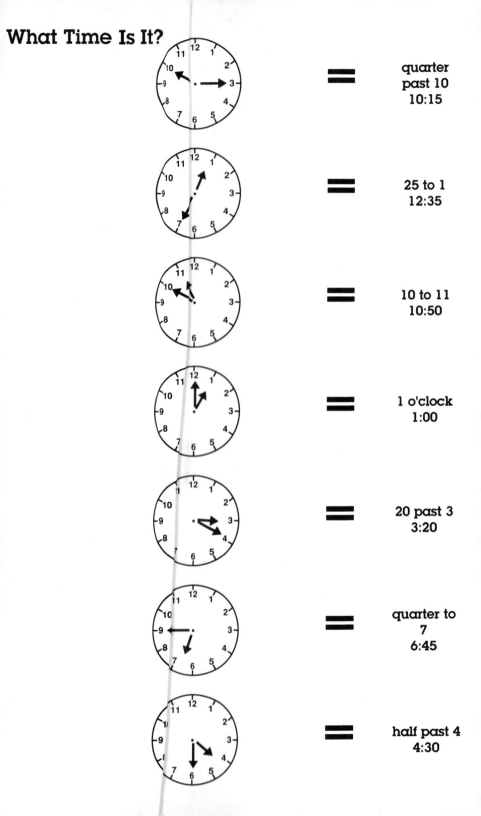

= quarter past 10
10:15

= 25 to 1
12:35

= 10 to 11
10:50

= 1 o'clock
1:00

= 20 past 3
3:20

= quarter to 7
6:45

= half past 4
4:30